NICK JR.

DORA the EXPLORER

I Love My Mami!

by Judy Katschke   illustrated by Dave Aikins

Ready-to-Read

Simon Spotlight/Nick Jr.

New York   London   Toronto   Sydney

Based on the TV series *Dora the Explorer*® as seen on Nick Jr.®

SIMON SPOTLIGHT
An imprint of Simon & Schuster Children's Publishing Division
1230 Avenue of the Americas,
New York, New York 10020
© 2006 Viacom International Inc.
All rights reserved. NICK JR., *Dora the Explorer,*
and all related titles, logos, and characters are registered trademarks of
Viacom International Inc.
All rights reserved, including the right of reproduction in whole or in part in any form.
SIMON SPOTLIGHT, READY-TO-READ, and colophon
are registered trademarks of Simon & Schuster, Inc.
Manufactured in the United States of America
First Edition
2 4 6 8 10 9 7 5 3 1
Library of Congress Cataloging-in-Publication Data
Katschke, Judy.
I love my mami! / by Judy Katschke; illustrated by Dave Aikins.—1st ed.
p. cm.
"Based on the TV series Dora the Explorer as seen on Nick Jr."
"#9."
Audience: Pre-level 1
Summary: Dora the Explorer spends a fun day with her mother.
ISBN-13: 978-1-4169-0650-6
ISBN-10: 1-4169-0650-9 (pbk.)
[1. Mothers and daughters—Fiction.] I. Aikins, Dave, ill. II. Title.
PZ7.K15665Il 2006
[E]—dc22
2005004048

Hi! I am Dora!

I am going to spend
the day with my **mami**.

First we feed the babies.

Then we make a
yummy breakfast.

My **mami** takes me
with her to work.

Look what I found!

Then **Mami** and I
go to the park.

We play on the swings.
Higher and higher we go!

I made a present
for **Mami.**

It is a picture of us!

Mami and I
had a great day.

I love my **mami**!
And **Mami** loves me.